TODAY'S HIP-HOP

by Lori Mortensen

CAPSTONE PRESS
a capstone imprint

Snap Books is published by Capstone,
1710 Roe Crest Drive, North Mankato, Minnesota, 56003.
www.mycapstone.com

Library of Congress Cataloging-in-Publication Data is available
on the Library of Congress website.
ISBN: 978-1-5435-5444-1 (library binding) — 978-1-5435-5448-9 (eBook PDF)

Summary: Provides information on the current trends and history of
hip-hop dance.

Editorial Credits
Gena Chester, editor; Kay Fraser, designer; Morgan Walters, media researcher;
Tori Abraham, production specialist

Photo Credits
Getty Images: David Livingston, bottom 23, FOX, top 17, top 21, Jenny Anderson,
29, NBC, 5, 6, 24, Theo Wargo, bottom 27; iStockphoto: Geber86, bottom 17;
Newscom: Rick Davis / Splash News, 9, Sthanlee B. Mirador_HHI / PRPP, bottom
21; Shutterstock: Africa Studio, 15, agsandrew, design element throughout, Albo, 12,
chaoss, Cover, 11, Debby Wong, 7, top 27, Gino Santa Maria, 13, bottom 19, julkirio,
design element throughout, Pavel L Photo and Video, top 19, ReVelStockArt, design
element throughout, SFROLOV, top 23, vladee, 25, ZenStockers, design element
throughout

Printed in the United States of America.
PA49

Table of Contents

CHAPTER 1

Hit the Floor

An army of dancers fills the stage. They're dressed all in black—caps, clothing, sneakers, and lipstick. Before they begin, their striking appearance captures the audience's attention. As they wait, anticipation builds.

A second later, they explode into movement. Hard. Fast. Clean. Rapid-fire hands flash, and legs kick in **unison**. Bodies leap up and down. Music pounds like bullets one minute, tinkling bells the next. "Blood, sweat, and tears!" a robotic voice proclaims. "I want to start a revolution." The 2017 Hit the Floor international dance competition is going full-throttle.

unison—matching movements perfectly

DM Nation competed in season 10 of America's Got Talent.

The explosive crew is DM Nation, an all-female hip-hop dance group from Quebec, Canada. The world first met them on *America's Got Talent* in 2015. The crew's high-energy performance brought the audience to its feet. DM Nation rocketed to first place at World of Dance Boston competition that same year. Their fast-paced, hard-hitting **choreography** has been astonishing crowds ever since. They're at the top of the hip-hop community as they take the dance form to new heights.

choreography—the arrangement of steps, movements, and required elements that make up a routine

DM Nation dance crew has a total of 14 dancers.

Fact

DM stands for District.mao, a dance studio in Quebec, Canada. Marie-Odile Haince-Lebel (far right) started the District.mao dance studio in 2005 when she was 19 years old.

CHAPTER 2

Hip-Hop Rewind

Hip-hop began in New York in the late 1970s. As **DJs** played funk and soul music, crowds danced in the mostly African-American neighborhoods. Dee-jaying, rapping, and graffiti painting were all part of this new cultural movement. One day, DJ Kool Herc tried something new. To make a **rhythm** "break" last longer, he used two **turntables**. When one rhythm section ended, he switched to the other one. This gave dancers twice as much time to dance. Kool Herc called the kids who danced during the break "b-boys," and "b-girls." It was the beginning of a new movement—hip-hop dance.

DJ—Disc Jockey; DJs play pre-recorded music for a radio, party, or club audience
rhythm—a pattern of beats, such as in music
turntable—a circular, revolving surface used to play records

Fact
DJ Kool Herc's real name is Clive Campbell. He moved from Jamaica to New York in the late 1960s at the age of 12.

DJ KOOL HERC

DJ Kool Herc didn't just spark a revolution in dance—he also paved the way for hip-hop music. While other DJs played their music, Herc rapped in rhyme to the beat. His rhythmic chants drove crowds onto the dance floor. Herc's massive sound system vibrated the dancers' bodies. They could literally feel the music. His new style inspired dancers to come up with new steps. Kool Herc is known as the founding father of hip-hop.

B-boys and b-girls began competing in one-on-one dance battles. To win they had to keep coming up with bigger, better moves. Soon they were wowing neighborhood crowds with headstands, leg sweeps, and shoulder spins.

The dance movement spread from New York. In California, dancers added their own style. It was called **popping** and **locking**. "Boogaloo" Sam Solomon, a young dancer in Fresno, California, invented popping. In this style, dancers quickly **contracted** and released their muscles. Close by in Los Angeles, a young art student named Don "Campbellock" Campbell created locking. To lock, dancers suddenly froze, or locked, in place. The West Coast style was also influenced by The Jackson Five, a popular boy band, and by futuristic movies inspired by aliens and robots. Soon, TV shows, music videos, and movies, such as *You Got Served* and *Step Up* spread hip-hop dancing around the world.

popping—making short, quick, and explosive movements
locking—freezing in a certain position after a fast movement
contract—tensing a muscle to create movement

Fact
Popular TV shows such as *World of Dance* and *So You Think You Can Dance* showcase today's hip-hop dance talent.

Power moves, such as the jackhammer, are crowd favorites.

CHAPTER 3

All the Right Moves

Dancers follow important steps before they dance. Loose, comfortable clothing not only lets dancers move, it adds to their style. Sweatpants, cargo pants, and loose-fitting jeans are great choices. On top, jerseys, T-shirts, tank tops, and sweatshirts work just fine. Shoes are equally important. Most hip-hop dancers wear sneakers.

Next, dancers take time to stretch, warm up, and get their body ready to move. Dancers put on some music, then slowly warm up. Sudden, extreme movements before warming up can cause injuries.If that happens, dancers may need days, weeks, or even months to recover.

Fact
Today's dancers take their style cues from popular hip-hop artists. The rapper Kanye West even has his own successful fashion line called Yeezy.

There are many ways to learn hip-hop. One way is learning from friends. That's how hip-hop began. Dancers got together and shared their moves with each other. Another way is through YouTube tutorials online. Experts provide step-by-step instructions for popular hip-hop steps. Dancers also take hip-hop classes at dance studios. Classes are a great way for dancers to get personal feedback from dance professionals.

Successful dancers stick with practice and training. It takes time for bodies to stretch and build strength and stamina. Professional dancers spend years working on their craft. In addition to taking classes, they find ways to perform. That could be in dance battles, competitions, talent shows, or theater productions. Then they're performing with a dance crew, teaching classes, and creating online tutorials.

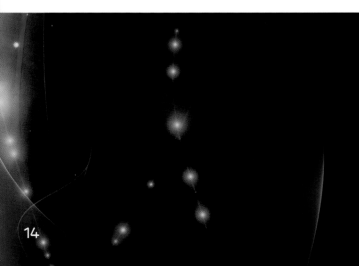

Dance classes aren't gender-specific, and hip-hop is popular among men and women.

CHAPTER 4

Hip-Hop Rocks

Hip-hop dance began in the streets. Dancers didn't need to look, act, or dress like formally trained dancers. All they needed was music, imagination, space, and plenty of attitude. Dance battles encouraged dancers to keep coming up with more amazing moves. New moves got new names. For example, steps performed while standing up are called toprock. Steps performed on the floor with hands and feet are called downrock, footwork, or floor work. Dancers came up with exciting steps such as the Soulja Boy, the SpongeBob, and the Running Man. Anyone could dance, invent, or add their own flavor to the hip-hop mix.

Hip-hop dancers continue to shape this popular dance form. French dancer Shaadow Sefiroth, South Korean Lee Jae Hyung "Poppin J," and Californian Mike Song are some of the best hip-hop dancers in the world. Their mastery of hip-hop and their unique style sets them apart. They show what else is possible.

TWITCH

Stephen "tWitch" Boss is one of the most famous and accomplished hip-hop dancers today. As a child he would pop and tick when he couldn't sit still, causing others to call him Twitch. This later influenced his stage name, tWitch.

After missing a spot in the top 20 in Season 3 of *So You Think You Can Dance*, he came back and finished runner-up in 2008's Season 4. He returned to the show in Season 7 as an All-Star dancer. His success didn't stop there. Since first getting his start on the reality show, he's a recurring guest DJ on *Ellen* and appeared in numerous dance movies.

In season 12 of So You Think You Can Dance, tWitch joined the show as a team captain for current contestants.

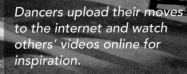

Dancers upload their moves to the internet and watch others' videos online for inspiration.

Power Up

One of the most challenging hip-hop steps is a power move. There are many different kinds. Windmills, head spins, jackhammers, flares, floats, and boomerangs are just a few. As the crowd looks on, it's like watching a dazzling acrobatic show.

The dancers make it look easy. But power moves require strength, balance, speed, and control. Strength so they can hold up their entire body. Balance so they don't topple over while they're spinning or hitting a pose. Speed so they can spin and move effortlessly from trick to trick. Control to do exactly as they please. If they are able to execute all five, they will successfully master a power move.

Fact
One of the more exciting moves is the Matrix, named after a scene in the movie franchise of the same name. From a standing position, without using their arms, dancers sink and slide backward onto the floor, then reverse the whole thing back up to standing.

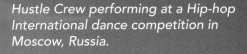

Hustle Crew performing at a Hip-hop International dance competition in Moscow, Russia.

HIP-HOP INTERNATIONAL

Hip-hop International, HHI, is one of the biggest series of hip-hop dance competitions in the world. Based in Los Angeles, co-founders Howard and Karen Schwartz got the idea when they saw street dancers in Paris and Tokyo. It inspired them to honor and unite the international hip-hop dance community.

In competitions, individuals and crews try to wow specially-trained judges. HHI competitions take place year-round in over 50 different countries. The biggest, called World Hip-hop Dance Championship, is an eight-day event. Over 4,000 dancers compete to win in the categories Breaking, Popping, Locking, and All Styles.

Popping

Popping is one of the most popular hip-hop styles. Dancers contract and release their muscles to the music. It looks like little jolts of electricity. South Korea's Hozin is one of the best poppers in the world. As he dances, his body shifts, jerks, and transforms in surprising and electrifying ways.

Locking

Locking is another popular hip-hop style. As dancers move, they suddenly freeze as if they're locked in place. Then, in a split second, the movement continues. Just like popping, this hip-hop style has a lot of exciting possibilities. In both styles, it's all about precision, control, and **isolation**. As dancers pop and lock, the audience watches to see where it will go next. In 2017, Florida's Dytto wowed crowds at World Dance Live with her precise and original performance.

Freestyling

Freestyling is a way of mixing it all up. Instead of performing set choreography, dancers make up movements as they go along. It's a popular style for dance battles. As dancers compete, they come up with bigger and better moves. Only the best will come out on top. France's Laurent and Larry Bourgeois, professionally known as "Les Twins," are two of the best. Freestyle workshops and competitions are held throughout the world.

isolation—moving individual parts of your body without moving the rest

JAJA

Jana "Jaja" Vankova from the Czech Republic is a well-known hip-hop dancer. She began dancing at age 14 in freestyle dance battles. In 2010, she joined I.aM.mE dance crew. With her help, the group won Season 6 of *America's Best Dance Crew*.

Since then, Jaja danced in the film *Step Up: All In*. She also competed in World of Dance Boston in 2017 with partner B-Dash. Their amazing choreography and pop-and-lock technique in their puppet routine wowed judges and fans.

Jaja also competed on So You Think You Can Dance *in season 12.*

Fact

Don "Campbellock" Campbell (far right) was a dance original. He invented the locking step and performed with his group, The Lockers.

CHAPTER 5

Show Stoppers

Dancers crowd into position on stage. In a flash, the lights go on and foot-thumping music fills the auditorium. The crew explodes into motion. The audience cheers. As the performance unfolds, it looks effortless. But great performances don't happen overnight. Memorable, show-stopping performances take months of planning. Each part fits together like pieces of a puzzle.

Choreography is a big piece of the puzzle. Dancers may be talented, but if their choreography is boring, the performance suffers. Good choreography has musicality, which means the moves match the music.

Skilled choreographers use stage direction, level changes, timing, and theme to their advantage. How dancers fill and move across the stage makes a difference. Changing levels from low to high adds variety. Movements may be fast, slow, or come to a complete stop. There may be one dancer or many dancers. Then choreographers use their movements to tell a story. Show-stopping performances use all of these things and leave the audience wanting more.

Dancers use many things to enhance a performance. Some even use water!

Fact

Tricia Miranda is one of the top hip-hop choreographers today. She's choreographed for music stars Missy Elliott and Beyoncé and on *So You Think You Can Dance* season 6. Her workshops and YouTube videos inspire dancers everywhere.

Costumes and Lighting

Costumes are another important part of the performance. For example, DM Nation is known for their militant black costumes and lipstick. It adds to their fierce, powerful style. When the Californian junior team Cubcakes Dance Crew appeared on *World of Dance* in 2018, they wore checkered T-shirts with pandas on the front. In each case, the costumes said something about the performers and set them apart. Lighting is another factor. The color and timing of the lights adds mood and meaning. *World of Dance, So You Think You Can Dance, and* Hip-hop International are great places to find top hip-hop performances.

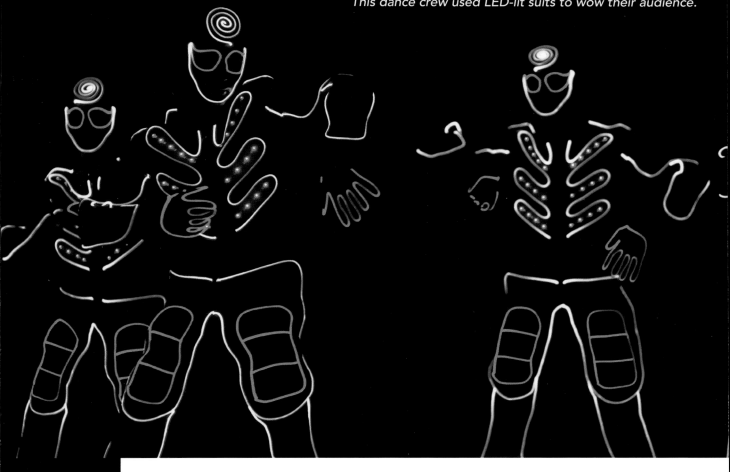

Rehearsals

Rehearsals give dancers a chance to perfect everything in their performance. Dancers not only need to memorize the choreography, they need to do it well. That means no extra hops, fidgets, or falls. It means performing in unison and rehearsing enough that a group of dancers move exactly alike. Dancers also need to make each movement important and intentional. This includes the transitions as well. Simple steps are just as important as the flashy ones.

25

CHAPTER 6

Hip-Hop Fusion

Today, hip-hop dancing is more popular than ever. What started on the streets of New York in the 1970s has spread around the world. Now, it's not just hip-hop. This popular style of dance is fusing with other arts in exciting ways.

One example of hip-hop fusion is Kenichi Ebina's style. Audiences saw the self-taught Japanese artist when he won Season 8 of *America's Got Talent* in 2013. His blend of sound, light, and visual effects with hip-hop, martial arts, and mime brought the audience to their feet. Today, Ebina performs and teaches all over the world. In 2017, he took over the Tokyo stage production of an anime classic, *Captain Tsubasas*.

Another example is the Grammy award-winning musical *Hamilton*. It is the story of Alexander Hamilton, one of America's Founding Fathers. Composer and playwright Lin-Manuel Miranda turned history on its head by fusing hip-hop with American history to tell Hamilton's story.

Fact

Hamilton is a Broadway sensation. Lin-Manuel Miranda got the idea while reading about Alexander Hamilton's humble beginnings and his brash personality. Miranda thought hip-hop's rebellious street style was the perfect way to bring Hamilton's American story to life for today's audience.

Kenichi Ebina

Hip-hop and ballet? Yes! Setting over 100 years of ballet tradition aside, The New Jersey Performing Arts Center showcased *The Hip-Hop Nutcracker*. It was their explosive version of Tchaikovsky's classic set in contemporary New York City. During the holiday season, it's performed at theaters across the country.

At the Chicago Multi-Cultural Dance Center (CMDC), there's Hiplet™ (pronounced hip-lay). In 2007, Homer Hans Bryant invented Hiplet™ by fusing classical ballet **en pointe** with hip-hop's fierce flair and style. It was the beginning of something BIG. After a CMDC Hiplet™ performance, the new style went viral on the social media. Since then, the dancers have done a TED Talk, TV commercial, and met with *Vogue* magazine.

No matter what form it takes, hip-hop continues to influence dancers and cultures around the world. As the pounding music plays, dancers move to the beat. Their bodies spin on the floor in a blur. Suddenly, their legs twist into the air and freeze. The crowd roars. It's exciting. It's fierce. It's hip-hop.

en pointe—style of dance performed in special shoes on the tips of the toes

Hiplet™ dancers at a pop-up performance in New York.

Glossary

choreography (kor-ee-OG-ruh-fee)—the arrangement of steps, movements, and required elements that make up a routine

contract (kuhn-TRAKT)—tensing a muscle to create movement

DJ (DEE-jay)—Disc Jockey; DJs play pre-recorded music for a radio, party, or club audience

isolation (eye-suh-LAY-shun)—moving individual parts of your body without moving the rest

locking (LAHK-ing)—freezing in a certain position after a fast movement

en pointe (POINT)—style of dance performed in special shoes on the tips of the toes

popping (POP-ing)—making short, quick, and explosive movements

rhythm (RITH-uhm)—a pattern of beats, such as in music

turntable (TURN-tay-buhl)—a circular, revolving surface used to play records

unison (YOO-nuh-sen)—matching movements perfectly

Read More

DeAngelis, Audrey and Gina DeAngelis. *Hip-Hop Dance*. Hip-Hop Insider. Abdo, 2018.

Jones, Jen. *Top Dance Tips*. Top Sports Tips. Capstone Press, 2017.

Lanier, Wendy Hinote. *Hip-Hop Dance*. Shall We Dance?. Focus Readers, 2017.

Internet Sites

Use Facthound to find Internet sites related to this book.

Visit www.facthound.com.

Just type in 9781543554441 and go!

 Check out projects, games and lots more at
www.capstonekids.com

Index